The Rabbi's Girls

BY THE SAME AUTHOR

Aldo Applesauce
Aldo Ice Cream
Baseball Fever
Busybody Nora
The Law of Gravity
Much Ado About Aldo
New Neighbors for Nora
Nora and Mrs. Mind-Your-Own-Business
Once I Was a Plum Tree
Superduper Teddy

The Rabbi's Girls

Johanna Hurwitz

illustrated by Pamela Johnson

William Morrow and Company
New York   1982

Printed in the United States of America.
2   3   4   5   6   7   8   9   10

Library of Congress Cataloging in Publication Data

Hurwitz, Johanna.
   The rabbi's girls.
   Summary: Moving to a new town, the birth of a sister, and the death of her rabbi father make 1923 a bittersweet year for eleven-year-old Carrie Levin.
   [1. Family life—Fiction. 2. Jews—United States—Fiction]
I. Johnson, Pamela, ill.   II. Title.
PZ7.H9574Rab   [Fic]   82-2102
ISBN 0-688-01089-X   AACR2

In memory of my grandparents,
Rabbi Israel and Esther Miller.

Contents

The
Rabbi's
Girls

1

Moving

This was not the first time and it would not be the last, I thought, when my younger sister Doris and I began to pack the dishes. We were preparing for another move. Less than two years before we had the same job when our family moved from Indiana to Illinois. Now here we were packing again, and in a couple of days we would be leaving for Lorain, Ohio.

Doris handed me a soup bowl, and I reached for a sheet of newspaper in which to wrap it. The black borders and the headline caught my eye. Dated August 3, 1923, the paper was a week old. *President Harding Dead!* the headline said. I thought of how shocked we had all been by the news. One moment Harding was the president of the United States, and the next moment Coolidge was president because Harding had died.

"Death does not respect titles," Papa said.

"Carrie Levin! Stop reading the old newspapers!" Doris scolded me. "We'll never finish at this rate."

We were wrapping and packing the milk dishes. Across the kitchen at the other cupboard, our older sisters, Abby and Betty, who were seventeen and fifteen, were packing the meat dishes. Evie, who was only six and the youngest in the family, was helping Mama pack the clothing. I suspected that Evie wouldn't be much of a help, but at least Mama didn't have to worry about things smashing to bits on the floor. Evie liked to do whatever Doris and I did, but we were older so of course we could do things that she couldn't.

Mama moved slowly. Her body was swollen out of shape because she was expecting another baby. We weren't permitted to talk about it much because of Mama's superstitions. She

worried about the evil eye, and so she thought that if no one spoke about the baby, which was due in just a few weeks, it would be better. Still, Doris and I sometimes wondered aloud if perhaps this time Mama would have a boy. Our family had five girls, and even though he never commented on it, we were sure that Papa would like to have a son. Having a brother would be nice. I liked the word and often said it to myself, practicing the sound. "This is my brother. . . . I have a brother. . . . My little brother. . . ." The baby would be something to look forward to when we got to Lorain.

"What's Lorain like?" I asked Papa.

"It's not so very different from here," he said. "About 50,000 people live there. Most of the men work in the steel mills or in the shipyards. The city is located right on Lake Erie," he added, pulling on his beard. "Learning new street names and meeting new people will seem a little strange at first, but before long we'll all feel at home." From his words, I knew he understood how I was feeling.

16

Since the day, two months before, when Papa and Mama told us that we would be leaving Rockford, my stomach had been in knots. It is hard to start over and over at new schools and to try and make new friends each time. Even though we had lived in five different places in my eleven years of life, the moving was always difficult.

"Are there many Jews?" Abby asked Papa.

"There are about 300," he said, smiling. "Many are shop owners. A few work in the mills. They don't all belong to the synagogue, but I'll see what I can do about that."

That was Papa's job. He was a rabbi, and it was the nature of his work that kept relocating our family every two or three years. I always had to explain to my Christian classmates that a rabbi is like a minister. Most of them had never heard of a rabbi before. "He marries people and conducts funerals and leads all the religious services at the synagogue," I would tell them. Then I had to stop and explain that a synagogue was like a church. Wherever we lived only a small percentage of people were Jewish. The Jewish customs and words always seemed strange to my classmates.

Of course, we were all very proud of Papa. It was an important honor, as well as a responsibility, to be a rabbi. "A rabbi has the hardest job in the world," Mama often said. "He has a hundred bosses."

"A rabbi should have only one boss," said Abby. "And that is God."

"You're right," agreed Mama. "But you are wrong."

Then she explained. "God is a good boss because he understands human nature and forgives errors. But on earth one has to answer to men as well. A rabbi is responsible to every member of his congregation. When he says Yes to one man, he may be saying No to another. Everyone has a different point of view, and it is hard to satisfy everyone at the same time."

I understood what Mama was saying. The idea was the same as in the Aesop's fable that I had read in one of my library books, the one about a miller and his son and a donkey. You cannot please everyone, and that was why Papa was forced to change jobs so often.

Poor Mama. If Papa had the hardest job in the world, then she had the second hardest. Each time we moved she had to supervise the packing and organize the actual departure while Papa went on ahead to find a place for us to live.

Sometimes, in the past, we had lived right in the synagogue building itself. That was awful, because we had to wear a freshly starched and ironed dress every day as if we were constantly having company. Luckily, the synagogue in Lorain did not have living quarters for us, and so Papa went on ahead and found a house on Brownell Avenue.

On the third Tuesday in August, we arrived in Lorain. As we got off the train, Evie shouted, "Look! There's another flag falling down!"

We all turned to look at where she had pointed.

19

"Evie," Betty said, "that flag is at half-mast, just like all the others we saw from the train window."

"It's to honor President Harding," I added. The newspapers said that flags had been lowered all over the country and even all over the world. Anyway, Lorain, Ohio, was not so far away from where Harding had been buried in his hometown of Marion, Ohio.

"It is not good to see so many signs of death," said Mama with a sigh, as we walked slowly up the street. Papa had hired an automobile to bring our luggage to the house, but we couldn't squeeze in with it. I looked at the buildings draped in black and hoped that Mama was wrong. I don't believe in all her superstitions, but I wished she wouldn't have these reminders of death while she was pregnant. Perhaps they would harm the new baby.

Then we arrived at the house on Brownell Avenue, and our thoughts were distracted from the gloomy signs of mourning.

"It's so tiny," Betty said, as we stood in the hot sun in front of the frame house. She was right. The house looked much smaller than the one we had just left behind. Then, before anyone had time to think what the smallness of the new house would mean in terms of rooms and beds and who would sleep where, Mama spoke.

"I love the porch!" she said, turning to Papa with a smile. "We never had a house with such a lovely porch before. I can't wait to sit on it."

I smiled at Mama. She had a way of always seeing the good in a bad situation. "We can play on it too," I said, running up the wooden steps. Doris followed behind me.

"It will be perfect for our games. It could be a ship or a castle," she agreed.

"Or else we can just sit here and read," I added, because reading is my favorite thing to do.

Papa showed us around the house. Though it was small, there was a good-sized backyard that would be big enough for a vegetable garden and for a chicken coop too.

While we were all standing out in the back, I thought I saw someone watching us through the fence that separated our yard from the one behind it. The person looked like a girl about my size, so I walked closer to get a better look. Whoever it was saw me coming and ran away.

"We can let the unpacking wait awhile," said Mama. "We'll live here long enough to put everything in its proper place."

Abby and Betty decided to walk into the city. They wanted to see where the high school was located since they would both be in classes there. Mama persuaded Evie to take a nap with her, and Papa had an appointment to meet someone at the synagogue. Doris and I were free to explore. It was an exciting moment, and we weren't sure which way to start off. I felt a little like those boys in the folktales who went off to seek their fortune. Should one turn right or should one turn left?

Then I thought of something. "Doris," I said,

"when we were standing in the backyard, I thought I saw a girl peeking at us through the fence."

"I didn't see anyone," said Doris.

Nevertheless, she agreed to walk around the block with me to see which house was behind ours. Perhaps we would find the girl there. As we walked, I could see the curtains moving in the windows of the houses that we passed. The housewives inside were peeking out to get a first glimpse of the new family. A woman sweeping her front walk nodded to us, but she didn't speak and neither did we.

Sure enough, just as I expected, sitting on the curb in front of the house that was behind ours was a girl just about our age. She was playing jacks.

"Hi," I said, trying to sound friendly and natural. Actually, I felt very shy, and my voice came out hoarse and almost in a whisper. "I'm Carrie Levin, and this is my sister Doris. We just moved here today. Could we play with you?"

"Are you twins?" the girl asked.

I laughed. "Everyone thinks we are, because Mama always makes us matching dresses," I explained. "Doris is as tall as I am, but I am a year older."

"Are you any good at jacks?" the girl asked us.

"Not too good," Doris admitted, "but it's still fun to play."

The girl smiled. "I'm very good. I'm the best in my class," she said. "Look," she demonstrated, clapping her hands three times and then picking up all the jacks with ease before the ball bounced on the ground.

Doris and I sat down on the curb beside her. "Would you teach us?" Doris asked.

"What's your name?" I asked her.

"Selena Edwards."

What a beautiful name, I thought. Like a princess in a fairy tale. I knew we would be good friends.

"That's my house," she said, nodding toward

24

the white frame one a few yards away. "I live right behind you."

"I saw you through the fence," I told her. "If we become friends, we can send messages back and forth from the windows. We can flash mirrors and things like that."

"That's a good idea," Selena said admiringly.

"I read it in a book," I admitted.

Selena handed the little ball to Doris and told her to take a turn. Doris succeeded in picking up each of the jacks. But when she tried to pick up two jacks at a time, she quickly missed.

"You have to scoop them up like this," said Selena, showing her the way to do it.

Doris tried again, even though it really wasn't her turn any longer. I didn't mind. I could hardly believe that less than two hours after we arrived in Lorain, I had found a friend. Wherever we lived, I had gone looking for one, but usually I hadn't been too successful.

Suddenly, a voice shouted from a window of the white house. "Selena! Come in at once!"

"Heck!" complained Selena. "That's my grandma. She lives with us, and she is always telling me to do something." She sighed. "I'll come right back. Don't go away."

"We just moved here today," I said, laughing. "We won't be leaving for a while, anyway." At that moment, I loved Lorain and hoped we would stay forever.

Doris practiced scooping up the jacks. She hadn't even reached threesie before Selena came out again.

"My grandma says that I can't play with you. You're dirty Jews," she said to us accusingly. She grabbed her jacks and ball from Doris and examined them carefully, as if she was looking to see what damage had been done to them by exposure to us.

"I thought we were going to be friends," Doris said.

I didn't say anything and held back the sob that was trying to escape from my throat. Grabbing Doris's hand, I slowly walked away. I wanted to run, but I wouldn't give Selena or her

26

grandmother, who was watching from the window, the satisfaction.

"I don't like that Selena Edwards," said Doris. "She's not very nice."

"We don't need her," I said to Doris, as I blinked back my tears. "We don't need anyone. I'm your friend and you are mine." I thought for a moment. "Don't tell Mama and Papa what happened. They have enough to worry about."

We had lost our desire to explore, so we returned to the house. The rest of the day was horrible. A dreadful woman named Mrs. Fromberg came to welcome us. I make fast judgments about people, and it only took a moment for me to decide that I disliked Mrs. Fromberg. She brought a noodle kugel made with cottage cheese and eggs for our first supper in our new home. The gesture was meant to be friendly, but we had to sit and listen to her talk for almost two hours. She was full of complaints about the old rabbi that Papa was replacing. I could imagine her speaking the same way about Papa in a year or two. Finally she left, and soon after Papa returned from the synagogue. Only then did I realize that Mrs. Fromberg had been waiting around in hopes of catching an early look at the new rabbi.

Abby and Betty found the crate with the appropriate dishes, and they unpacked enough for everyone to eat supper. Mrs. Fromberg's kugel was not nearly as tasty as Mama's, but since I didn't have any appetite that evening, it really didn't matter.

Mama noticed. "It looks as if the excitement of the move has filled you more than the food," she said. I just nodded my head. It was better to let Mama think that. She would find out soon enough what an awful place we had moved to. I hated Lorain.

2

Lorain

By the time all the boxes were unpacked, the pictures hung on the walls, and the old curtains adjusted to fit the new windows, it was time for school to begin for us girls. This year even Evie was old enough to attend. She was in the first grade, and she walked proudly next to Doris and me. I was in the fifth grade. Usually once the newness of school was over, I loved school. But from the very first day, I knew I would hate school in Lorain. Selena Edwards was in my class.

There was one good thing about Lorain, however. The public library was larger and open longer hours than the one we had left behind in Rockford. We had been living in

Lorain only two days before we made this discovery and got our membership cards. Once or twice a week, I would go with Doris and bring home a new supply of books to read. Then I devised a new way of walking to and from school. I walked with my head stuck inside a book. Of course, I wouldn't have been able to manage without Doris and Evie, who walked on either side and guided my steps. That way I could become absorbed in a story and not worry about walking into a tree or stumbling off a curb. I also didn't have to worry about meeting Selena.

"You could get hit by an automobile," Mama said. "Every day there are more automobiles on the streets than the day before."

"Yes. Everyone has an automobile but us," Betty complained.

On the afternoon of September 6, Mama wasn't waiting out on the porch to greet us as she usually did. Instead, Abby was standing there, and she had big news.

"Mama had the baby," she announced. "It's a girl!"

I dropped my library book in surprise. "Today?" I gasped.

"I came home from school at noon," Abby explained to us. "I had a feeling that Mama would need me, and I was right. So I called the synagogue, and I spoke with Mrs. Fromberg, who told me to call Miss Libby. She's a nurse, and she helps whenever new babies are born around here."

I sat down on the porch steps with Doris and Evie and thought about the news. Another sister. What a disappointment! I had hoped we'd have a brother. "Did you know Mama was going to have the baby today?" I asked the others. I couldn't imagine something so momentous happening without more warning.

"Look who's coming," said Evie, pointing down the street. We all turned to look. Unfortunately, it was not Betty, who was still walking home from the high school, or Papa. It was Mrs. Fromberg.

"I didn't want to use the telephone. I was afraid the ringing would disturb your poor mama," she said. "So I came as quickly as I could. Your papa is busy arranging for a funeral. Old Mrs. Rabinowitz passed away this morning. I told him about the baby, and he'll come home as soon as he can," Mrs. Fromberg reported officiously. She had been helping Papa a few hours a week by writing letters and answering the telephone at the synagogue.

We sat on the porch listening to Mrs. Fromberg. There were not many Jewish families in our part of town, and we missed having Jewish neighbors. So it seemed very bad luck that Mrs. Fromberg was the one we did have.

"Another girl," said Mrs. Fromberg, sighing and shaking her head. "Your poor father. I told your mother that she should eat the heel of the bread each Shabbos. It worked for me. I have two wonderful sons."

I bit my lip to keep from speaking rudely to Mrs. Fromberg. Whether Mama had a girl or a boy was none of her business.

"Papa says he loves girls just as much as boys," said Abby calmly.

"Of course, of course," said Mrs. Fromberg. "But every man needs a son to say prayers for him when he dies. Both my sons said them for my husband, may he rest in peace."

"Girls can say them too," I blurted out. "Girls are just as important in the world as boys." I felt my face turning red. Mrs. Fromberg had a way of saying things that always made me mad.

"We shouldn't be worrying about prayers for the dead now," said Abby gently. "This is a birth in our family, not a death."

"A birth, but not a bris," rejoined Mrs. Fromberg with a sigh. She was referring to the ritual ceremony that was performed in Jewish families after the birth of a son. She seemed determined to be unhappy about the new baby.

No wonder it was so hard to like Mrs. Fromberg. "She is more religious than God," Betty had told us, and we all agreed with her. She was always worrying about whether a pot was kosher or how a law should be interpreted. She bothered Papa constantly for advice. I sometimes suspected that she was checking up on our family too. Twice she stopped Evie in the street to ask her what she had eaten for lunch. She acted as if she was trying to catch us breaking one of the religious laws.

Mama laughed and began referring to her as Mrs. Froomberg, because *froom* is a Yiddish word that means very religious. Papa shrugged his shoulders and said that Mrs. Fromberg meant well. He never said anything unpleasant about anyone. After all a rabbi has to be understanding.

"Well, Evie. You won't be the baby anymore," said Mrs. Fromberg, bending over and running her hands through Evie's dark, curly hair.

"I'm a big girl now," said Evie proudly, rolling her eyes at Mrs. Fromberg. "I'm six years old."

As she spoke, I realized that Evie had been the family baby longer than any of us girls. I couldn't even remember life before Doris was born, though I do have a few memories from before Evie's birth. I hoped Evie would accept the new baby well. She was used to being petted and spoiled by everyone.

"I must go home to cook supper for my sons," said Mrs. Fromberg. "I'll be back tomorrow to see if I can help in any way," she threatened, as she started off down the street.

From the opposite direction, Betty came walking toward us. When she saw Abby on the porch, she called out, "Where were you? I've been standing around all this time waiting!"

Abby ignored the question and shared her news instead. "Mama just had a baby girl," she said. We all watched as the expression on Betty's face changed. Obviously, she was just as surprised as I had been.

"If there is one thing this family doesn't need, it's another girl," said Betty crossly.

"Thank you, Mrs. Fromberg," said Abby sarcastically, which was not at all like her.

"Where's Mama?" asked Evie.

"She's upstairs in bed. Where did you think she would be?" asked Doris, who had hardly said a word since we arrived home from school.

"She's resting now," Abby explained. "But Miss Libby says we can go up and see her and the baby in a little while."

We sat on the porch steps, each digesting the news in her own way. It wasn't every day that you went off to school and returned home to discover a new addition to your family.

"What do you think we'll name the baby?" I asked, turning to the others. Immediately everyone was offering suggestions.

"It has to start with *F*," Doris reminded us.

Mama and Papa have insisted that they hadn't intended to name us in alphabetical order by birth, but that is how it worked out with the first three, and afterward the practice continued. Jewish children are named after relatives who have died. It is a way of honoring their memory. So when their first child was born, Papa and Mama named her Abigail after Mama's own mama who had passed away in

Russia. Next came Bluma, whom we call Betty and who got her name from Papa's mama, who also died in Russia. (When I was younger, I always assumed that Russia must have an unhealthy climate. All our Russian relatives were dead ones.) I was named for Papa's Aunt Chava, and since we were living in North Carolina when I was born, they called me Carolina, or Carrie for short. Next came Doris, who was named for Aunt Devorah, and Evie, named for Papa's sister Eva. Betty, hating her name of Bluma, had given all of us our American nicknames. It was funny how they stuck so well. But sometimes Papa or Mama would forget and call us by our Hebrew names instead.

We heard the sound of the baby crying inside the house. "That's baby F," said Doris. "She sounds just as noisy as Evie did."

"I was noisier than baby F," insisted Evie. "I can remember!"

"You can't remember when you were a baby," said Doris.

"Yes, I can," Evie insisted, whining.

"Never mind," said Abby. "Look who's coming!"

We all turned and faced the street. This time Papa was walking toward the house. You could recognize him a block away, because he looked so different from the other men in the area. He always wore a necktie and a felt hat instead of the cloth cap that the other men wore. Of course, his beard added to his different, distinctive look too. He always appeared important. We all ran down the street to greet him. Papa had a huge smile on his face. He certainly didn't seem disappointed not to have a son. Too bad Mrs. Fromberg wasn't around to see him now, I thought.

"What are we going to name the baby?" asked Evie, nodding toward the house. "We didn't get a chance to think of some *F* names."

"She'll be named after my sister Lila," said Papa. "In Hebrew, her name will be Lila, which means night. But Mama and I thought we would call her Lorain in English."

"But that is *L*, not *F*," I protested.

"Where is it written that children must be named in alphabetical order?" asked Papa. "She'll be the last. There will be no more daughters or sons for Mama and me. Six children is a big family."

He paused, stroking his graying beard, and said thoughtfully, "In any event, *L* is a fine letter, and even though we have only been in Lorain a few weeks, it seems like a fine place. Perhaps we shall stay here a long time. I think Lorain will be a fine name for your new sister."

"Then she'll be named after a place, just as I am," I said. I am very proud to have the name of an American state, even if I have almost no memories of life in North Carolina.

"Thank goodness you didn't name me after the place where I was born," Betty said. She had been born in Milwaukee, Wisconsin. "That would be even worse than Bluma."

From inside the house, we could hear the cries of the baby.

"Come," said Papa. "Let us go inside and

meet your new sister and my daughter. She seems like a noisy one."

"Yes," I said, pushing the front door open for the others. "Let's go and meet Lorain Levin!" And for once, I was so excited that I forgot my library book out on the porch.

3

A Wedding

Rosh Hashanah, the Jewish New Year, occurred when Baby Lorain was only five days old. Mama was pleased that the baby had been born early. "It could be bad luck to be born on Yom Kippur," she said, referring to the very solemn holiday that came ten days after Rosh Hashanah. Because of the new baby, Mama was not strong enough to attend the holiday services, but she supervised everything in the house from her bed. We went off wearing our new outfits, which Mama had made for us during the summer.

I knew that more people were looking at us than were studying the Hebrew words in the prayer book during the services. Afterward everyone came up to greet us and to look us over at close hand.

"Well, Abby," said one elderly woman, speaking to Betty, "the rabbi's girls have increased the Jewish population of Lorain."

I looked at Betty. If there is one thing she really hates, it is the way people lump us together. "It's as if we had no identities," she says crossly. "The rabbi's girls. The rabbi's girls. I want to be known for myself."

Mixing up our names doesn't bother any of the rest of us. In fact, I always think it's funny, and besides I'm proud to be one of the rabbi's girls.

From bed, Mama had instructed Abby and Betty as they prepared the holiday foods. They made several round loaves of challah bread to signify that the year is round. And they made honey cake for a sweet new year. In the afternoon, several members of the congregation came to visit us. Some brought little gifts for Mama and the new baby. Of course, Mrs. Fromberg came. Hardly a day passed that she didn't stop by. She almost seemed to want to become part of our family. Mama explained that she had been widowed shortly before we arrived in Lorain. Her sons were grown men, and although they still lived at home, they needed her less and less. So even though I didn't care for her, I had to tolerate her presence.

One of the visitors that day was Dr. Mandelbaum. He was president of the board of trustees at the synagogue, and he had conducted the vote when they decided to give Papa the job here in Lorain. Dr. Mandelbaum's wife was spending the holidays with her parents in Cleveland, but the doctor's son accompanied his father to our house.

From the first moment, I disliked them both. Dr. Mandelbaum seemed filled with his own importance, and his son seemed just as pompous. Danny Mandelbaum was a little older than Abby. He talked to her, telling her that he was going off to the University of Chicago in February. To me, his words sounded unnatural, as if he had practiced them at home before he said them aloud. I was surprised that Abby seemed to like him. She served him an extra large slice of the honey cake, and she blushed whenever she spoke to him.

When the holidays were over, people started coming to Papa for advice. If a child wasn't doing well in school, the matter would be discussed with the rabbi. If a woman had a disagreement with her mother-in-law, or if a man lost his job and was looking for work, they would come to the rabbi. Everyone was sure that the rabbi could help him during his time of trouble. That was what he was paid for after all. Mama was right. Papa's job was indeed a hard one.

One autumn afternoon, when Lorain was just two months old, Doris, Evie, and I came home from school to find Papa sitting in the front room with one of his bar mitzvah students. We stood outside on the porch, listening. The boy was approaching his thirteenth birthday. Soon he would be called to read from the Torah, and he had to learn to chant the prayers in the special way that it had been done from generation to generation. Papa's violin was nearby. Whenever a boy had difficulty with a melody that he should be chanting, Papa would accompany him on the instrument. I had heard that sound many, many times before in each of the cities where we had lived.

"I wonder how many boys have learned the sacred words and harmonies from Papa?" I asked Doris and Evie. Of course, they couldn't answer my question.

"Papa has a wonderful voice," said Doris. "Mama says he could have been an opera singer if he had had the money to study music at a conservatory when he was young."

"Then who would have been the rabbi?" asked Evie.

I shrugged my shoulders. She was right. It was important that Papa be the rabbi. Abby had inherited Papa's musical talent. She played the piano, and sometimes in the evenings, if there were no visitors in the house and no calls

on the telephone for Papa, the two of them would play duets. I loved to sit and listen, as if I were at a concert.

As we opened the door to enter the house a wonderful smell filled the air. Mama was baking. We tiptoed into the kitchen so as not to disturb Papa and his student or Lorain, who was sleeping.

"Oh, can I have one?" I cried out. Mama was making rugalach, which were my favorite treat.

"Just one each," said Mama. "We're having company tonight, and I want to serve them."

"Who's coming?" I asked, as I bit into the warm pastry with cinnamon and raisins.

"There's going to be a wedding."

"Oh, I love weddings," I said, "and this will be our first here in Lorain." From time to time, Papa performed marriages in our home for people who wanted small, private ceremonies.

"I want you girls to help me straighten up as soon as Papa finishes his lesson. I want everything to look perfect."

"Everything looks perfect to me," Doris said, and I agreed.

"Not perfect enough," said Mama. "Evie, you keep an eye on Lorain," she said, pointing to the baby asleep in her cradle. "Doris, take this dustcloth and get into all the corners."

"What will I do?" I asked.

"You'll help me move the furniture," said Mama. "Abby has a piano lesson this afternoon, and Betty is staying after school for something too."

When Papa's student left, Mama and I pushed all the chairs back close to the walls to make the living room seem larger. When we finished, I helped her set the table and get the supper ready.

"I'll never get married in someone's living room," said Betty, when we sat down to eat. "I want a fancy wedding like the ones in the moving pictures. And I'll wear a long, white gown too." All of us girls loved going to the moving pictures, but Betty seemed to be the most influenced by what she saw. She was always fantasizing about how someday she would move to New York City and do glamorous things.

"Don't spill anything on the tablecloth," Mama instructed. "Tomorrow is laundry day, and the extra tablecloth and sheets aren't clean." We were having herring and boiled potatoes for supper. There were also cucumbers and tomatoes, the last of the fresh produce that had been given to us from someone's garden. For dessert there were stewed prunes. Everyone was careful, but at the last moment Evie spilled a little of the juice from the fruit on the tablecloth.

"Oh, Evie," scolded Doris. "Look what you did!"

"Never mind," said Mama. "What can't be helped shouldn't upset us. The couple will be just as married with a spot on the cloth as without it. The important thing is that they will have a proper Jewish ceremony." She smiled proudly at Papa.

Papa went and changed his shirt and combed

his hair. He looked more distinguished than ever when he reappeared wearing his white silk prayer shawl over his shoulders. I helped Abby clear the table and then went and combed my hair while Betty and Abby finished washing up for Mama, who was nursing Lorain.

We were all ready when the knock sounded at the door. Abby went to open it. Standing in the doorway was a young man about twenty and a young woman who looked about Abby's age.

"Is this the home of Rabbi Levin?"

"Come in. Come in," Papa called out. He shook hands with the young couple. The groom was named Jack. His bride-to-be was Sylvia. "Didn't you bring a witness?" asked Papa, looking around. "There must be another man present before I can perform the ceremony."

The young man looked flustered. "I didn't think of it," Jack said.

Papa tugged at his beard, and we all stood about waiting to hear what he would say. "Let me think," said Papa. "Perhaps I can call someone." As we stood waiting there was a knock at the door. Papa raised his eyebrows in puzzlement. He wasn't expecting anyone else this evening. I went to open the door. To my surprise, Danny Mandelbaum was standing on the doorstep. I wondered why he had come.

"I brought this book of my father's," he said stiffly. "Your father expressed a desire to read it." From the way he was peering in through the door, I realized that he was hoping to catch a glimpse of Abby. I wanted to grab the book and close the door, but Papa came up behind me.

"Why, Danny, what wonderful timing!" said Papa, holding out his hand to shake Danny's. "I'm always glad to see you," Papa said, "but tonight I am especially glad." He put his arm around Danny and drew him into the house. "You will be a witness at an important event."

Danny's presence almost spoiled the evening for me. We needed a witness, but why did it have to be him, I wondered, as Abby, Betty, Doris, and I each took a corner of the tablecloth and then stood on one of the dining-room chairs.

Jewish couples are married under a canopy, and that evening the tablecloth with the prune-juice stain was going to serve as the canopy, or "chuppa," as it is called in Yiddish.

Abby looked at Danny Mandelbaum and smiled. Evie stood watching with Mama. Only Lorain was missing; she was asleep again in her cradle. The bridegroom and Danny each put on a skullcap that Papa gave them. Papa's head was already covered. Even in the house he always wore something on it. Jack took Sylvia by the arm, and together they walked under the canopy.

Papa began to recite the marriage ceremony in Aramaic. I loved to hear his voice even when I couldn't understand the words. Sometimes it seemed as if Papa was an actor in a play in another language.

After a few minutes, my arm began to get tired, but I still held it high. The groom drank wine from a glass, which meant that the ceremony would soon be concluded. Papa wrapped the wineglass in a cloth napkin and put it on the floor. The groom lifted his foot and stamped down on it. Papa said that the breaking of the glass symbolized the destruction of the Temple. Next the couple kissed one another, just like a couple in the moving pictures. Papa shook the groom's hand. *"Mazel tov,"* he said. "May you have a long and happy life together."

The actors stepped out from under the canopy, and we could get off our chairs. The play was over. I helped Doris put the cloth carefully back on the table. By pulling it slightly to one side, we fixed it so the stain didn't show. Anyhow, I didn't think the couple would notice or be concerned if they did. As for Danny Mandelbaum, I didn't care what he thought. Mama lit the stove under the coffeepot and brought the plate of rugalach to the table.

We sat down at the table. Danny managed to sit next to Abby, and he looked pleased with himself. The good smell of the coffee and the sweet taste of the pastries relaxed everyone, and I forgave Danny Mandelbaum for his presence at our special evening. I wished I was as old as Abby and Betty and could drink straight coffee. I liked its bitter taste. My cup was half coffee and half milk. It seemed so babyish.

Sylvia bent down to look at Lorain sleeping in her cradle. "She is so pretty," she said. "Like a little doll."

"You mean the ribbon is pretty," corrected Mama, pointing to the red sash on the top of the cradle. I smiled at Abby across the table. Mama was so superstitious that she never let anyone admire her children. She always said things like, "I have not six daughters," when she meant the opposite. She was afraid of tempting the evil eye.

Everyone finished the coffee. Now the bride and groom would go off to live happily ever after, I thought. I looked at Abby. Next June she would be graduating from high school. She was old enough to get married too. Mama had already been married when she was seventeen.

Trying to imagine Abby standing under a chuppa was hard. Maybe someday she might stand there next to Danny Mandelbaum. Did Abby think about that too? I didn't want her to get married and certainly not to him. She should stay home and hold up the chuppa with the rest of us. I liked the way things were, and I didn't want our family to change. Ever.

4

Arithmetic

At the end of November, my teacher, Miss Peterson, changed all the seating around in the classroom.

"Now that I know who my star pupils are, I want them to help me," she said, and she began pairing the brighter students with the slower ones. I was proud to get a seat in the front row. But my delight was changed to embarrassment when the student assigned to sit beside me was Selena Edwards.

The two of us had not exchanged a single word since that first afternoon our family arrived in Lorain. Fortunately, Selena's grandmother's prejudice took the form of ignoring us. And none of our other neighbors showed any outward signs of hostility. Everyone on the street nodded to us, and one or two even came by to have a peek at the new baby. All people love new babies.

I wondered if Selena would ask Miss Peterson to change her seat again. Miss Peterson was a strict teacher, but she was also fair. The first week of school she had taken points off my arithmetic test because I had put my name in the right-hand corner of the page as I had been taught to do in Rockford. Here in Lorain, children were supposed to put their name in the left-hand corner of the page. She also deducted points on the spelling test because I wrote my name as Carrie instead of Carolina. "Imagine," said Miss Peterson. "There was only one paper without errors, but the student couldn't spell her own name!" You can be sure that by the second week of school my name was properly spelled on every paper the way Miss Peterson expected it.

Miss Peterson did not show partiality to children of any one nationality as teachers sometimes did. (One advantage—and disadvantage—of attending as many schools as I had was that I had been exposed to the quirks of many different teachers.) The children in the class were of every background: Ukrainian, German, Italian, French, Irish, Hungarian, and many, many more. Miss Peterson said that Lorain and our classroom were just like the rest of America—a big melting pot. Yet even if there were many backgrounds represented in my class, they were all Christian, which gave them a common bond. The 300 or 400 Jews in town were scattered about. I was the only Jew in my class, and so I always felt a bit of an outsider, just as Doris and Evie were in their classes.

I watched Selena's face when Miss Peterson told her where to sit. Selena didn't say a word. She came and put her books inside her desk, but she didn't look at me. Perhaps she would have her mother write a note and bring it to school the next day.

When the time came for arithmetic, Miss Peterson wrote ten examples on the blackboard. The chalk squeaked against the slate and caused me to shudder. Selena giggled. "I hate that sound," she whispered. I was amazed that she had spoken to me.

"No speaking. I want silence now," called Miss Peterson without turning around. She continued writing the examples on the board. "Now," said Miss Peterson, once again facing the class, "you will work as partners. My star math students may speak as they help their new seatmates do this assignment. But you can only talk about arithmetic," she warned.

I copied the first example on my sheet of paper. It was simple division with decimals. "Can you do this one?" I asked Selena.

Selena shrugged her shoulders and started to copy the example too. Then she began chewing on her pencil as she tried to figure out the answer.

"Watch how I do it," I whispered. Speaking in class—especially with Selena after all these weeks—seemed strange. I showed her how to move the decimal point before doing the dividing. The decimals didn't change the problem at

all. Very slowly Selena began to attempt to figure it out.

After she got the answer to the first example, I encouraged her to go on to the next. Selena looked exhausted. How could someone be so agile with a ball and jacks but hardly be able to move a pencil on a sheet of paper and write the answer to a simple arithmetic example!

By the time the arithmetic period was over, I was exhausted too. Explaining the same thing over and over without losing patience was not easy. Still, I felt proud that I had been selected to help with the lesson. I had always thought that I would like to be a teacher when I grew up. This work was good practice for me.

As we put our papers away and got ready to line up for recess, Selena whispered, "Wouldn't my mom be surprised if I got an A in arithmetic. Last time I got a D. I always get a D in arithmetic and an A in spelling." It was true that Selena, despite her poor math ability, was one of the best spellers in the class. That someone could be so good and so bad at the same time seemed strange.

"Even if you got a C it would be an improvement," I pointed out. I doubted that Selena would ever get an A in arithmetic. My teaching wasn't that good. I was surprised that she didn't resent having me coach her in her schoolwork. As if to answer my thoughts, Selena said, "I won't tell my grandma that I'm sitting next to you. That way we can be friends and she won't know." She reached out and squeezed my hand. A feeling of warmth and happiness filled me. Selena really wanted to be my friend. Her grandmother was the one who was preventing us from playing together.

Out in the school yard, Selena asked me, "Do you want to go to the movies with me on Saturday? They are showing *The Hunchback of Notre Dame* with Lon Chaney. We could meet there, as if by accident, and then sit together and watch the picture."

I was overjoyed by the invitation, but then I

realized I couldn't accept. "I can't go to the movies on a Saturday. It is our Sabbath, and it is forbidden. But I could go with you on a Sunday."

"What do you mean?" asked Selena, looking puzzled.

"My parents wouldn't let me go on a Saturday," I explained again patiently, as I had the arithmetic problems. Selena seemed to have to hear everything two or three times before she could really understand. "There are certain things that Jewish people can and cannot do on the Sabbath. I can take a walk, but I can't spend money. Papa allows us to go to the library and even to carry home an armful of books, although some Jewish people wouldn't even do that. But he says that reading is sacred, and so he permits it. Movies are strictly forbidden. I can't go on a Saturday, but sometimes, when Doris and I have the money, we go on Sunday," I said.

"You're lying. You just don't want to be my friend after all," accused Selena.

"I don't tell lies," I said, beginning to get angry. I had wanted to be Selena's friend in the worst way, but if she was going to be so difficult, perhaps her friendship wasn't worth the effort.

"How come your sister is allowed to go to the movies on Saturday then?" demanded Selena.

"What do you mean?" I asked her. "No one in my family goes to the moving pictures on Saturday!"

"I've seen your sister there many times. So there!" said Selena.

"That's impossible," I said. But then I thought a moment. "Which sister?" I asked her.

"The one with the long, dark hair."

"Betty?" I shook my head. "You must have mistaken someone else for her. Lots of girls have long, dark hair."

"I recognized her coat," said Selena. "I'm not that dumb. Just because I can't do arithmetic doesn't mean that I wouldn't recognize your sister. And I know when someone doesn't want to be my friend," she said, turning and walking over to a group of girls jumping rope. In a

65

moment, she was jumping too. I stood by myself and tried to figure out what Selena had said. None of it made any sense. Or did it? I would have to speak with Betty when I got home.

"Yes," said Betty defiantly, when I hesitatingly brought up the subject. "Sometimes, when I have the money, I go to the moving pictures on Saturday. Why shouldn't I?"

"But, Betty, we're Jewish. We're not supposed to. What will Papa say if he finds out?" I whispered. Even though we were alone, I could barely make myself speak aloud.

"I suppose you're going to tell him!" accused Betty.

"No," I said. "That's not what I meant. I just don't understand how you can break the Sabbath. Aren't you worried that God is watching you and that he will punish you?"

"If there is a God, and I'm not so sure there is," said Betty, "he has bigger things on his mind. Or at least he should. There are people in the world who are starving or dying. There are people oppressed by their bosses. So what if I go to a movie? It doesn't hurt anyone, and it gives me a little pleasure." She paused for breath. "Mr. Lewis, my history teacher, says that religion is the opiate of the masses. We're living in a modern era, and we should be ruled by the laws of socialism. We should learn to share and treat one another as equals, but as long as we live by the archaic rules of religion, this will never be."

"Betty," I said, "I don't understand half of what you're saying. Aren't you afraid that Papa will find out? I won't tell him, but someone is sure to see you standing on line to buy your movie ticket." I paused for a moment thinking. "If Mrs. Fromberg found out, it would be all over Lorain in an hour."

"That's my problem. Don't worry about me. I can take care of myself," said Betty. "Just don't say anything. If I say that I'm going to visit a friend on Saturday afternoons, that's all you know, understand?"

I nodded. Betty is the one member of our

family who has made friends wherever she has gone. No wonder none of us had doubted her stories about visiting friends on Saturday afternoons. Still, I was badly troubled. I didn't understand how you could break laws that you had observed since the moment you were born. Jewish laws were part of a tradition hundreds and hundreds of years old. Being Jewish had always made our family outsiders among our Christian neighbors, but still we were proud of our heritage that linked us to ancient and grander times. It was as if Moses and Abraham were distant relatives too far back to count. They were grandfathers with more *greats* in front of their names than one could say in a single day, but still they were our ancestors. That was how Papa had taught us to see them.

Later, pushing Lorain up and down the street in the baby buggy, I thought about the problem still more. Lorain was cuddled under so many blankets that only the tip of her nose showed. Even though I was wearing a sweater under my coat, I shivered as the wind blew from Lake

Erie. Staying a baby would be better, I thought, watching Lorain. Then one wouldn't have problems to worry about. I walked to the end of the street, turned the carriage around, and went in the opposite direction. As I stopped to adjust the cover under Lorain's chin I saw that she was smiling in her sleep. I wondered if babies had dreams.

"Carrie," a voice called me. I turned around. Abby was just crossing at the corner. She had gotten a part-time job working at the pharmacy, and she worked there most afternoons after school let out. "Hi, honey," she said, smiling at me.

Abby always had a smile on her face, but today she looked especially radiant. "How was your work?" I asked her.

"It was fine," Abby said. "Danny Mandelbaum came into the store this afternoon to pick up some things for his father. We had a long talk. He says that he doesn't want to go into medicine. He wants to become a lawyer. Isn't that wonderful?"

Nothing about Danny Mandelbaum seemed wonderful to me. I wasn't even sure what a lawyer did. But Abby's delight was infectious. Everything seemed straightforward and simple to Abby. She didn't have any problems. Too bad one couldn't jump from being an infant like Lorain to being full grown like Abby. Being eleven and a half was what was hard, I decided.

5

Bad Times

As always winter brought more than cold weather. It brought sickness too. One by one we all caught our annual winter colds. Half the children in Evie's class had been home sick. The students in the higher grades didn't stay home unless they had high fevers, but everyone at school was sneezing and coughing and blowing noses into cotton handkerchiefs.

Selena was absent for several days, and I thought that she was ill. Then one morning Miss Peterson announced to the class that the reason for her absence was that her grandmother had died of pneumonia. Even though I hated her grandmother, I felt sorry for Selena. All the students made sympathy cards to send to Selena and her family. I decorated mine with flowers and birds and signed it "Your friend, Carrie." I underlined the word friend two times, hoping Selena would understand that I didn't hold any grudges.

When I came home from school, I told Mama about Selena's grandmother. Immediately she took a fresh loaf of bread that was still warm from the oven and wrapped it in a clean towel. She also took a jar of strawberry jam that she had made when we were still living in Rockford. "Come," she said. "We must pay a sympathy call. They are our neighbors." So even though Mama had never spoken to anyone in the Edwards family, she put on her coat and went around the block with me.

The Edwardses seemed surprised to see Mama and me. But they accepted the gifts, and Mama comforted Mrs. Edwards. Selena and I sat side by side smiling shyly at one another. One would never guess that we sat together at school. When we said good-bye, Mrs. Edwards and Mama hugged one another like old friends.

72

Grown-ups were unpredictable, I thought, as I watched them.

The cold weather continued all during January. Every day the temperature was below freezing, and each morning Abby got up early and went to the basement to fill the furnace with coal. The heat came up slowly, and even in our union suits we shivered with the cold. Betty complained that the long underwear beneath her clothes made her look fat. But none of us, including Betty, would have considered going outside or even staying inside without the added protection that the union suits gave us on bitter cold days.

We older girls recovered from our colds. But Lorain didn't. She had a little cough, and her nose was stuffed up. "If only she knew how to blow her nose," I said, watching her little body tossing and fretting in her bed.

"Five-month-old babies can't blow their noses," said Abby with a sigh, as she picked her up. Lorain seemed to breathe better when she was upright rather than lying on her back, so

73

Abby carried her on her shoulder many hours during the day.

Mama heated kettles of water and hoped that the steam in the kitchen air would help to clear Lorain's head. And finally, when the cold persisted still longer, Dr. Mandelbaum came to the house. For Mama and Papa to summon the doctor meant that they were really worried. Even when Evie had the measles the year before and her temperature rose to 105, they didn't call a doctor. Mama always said that if you ate well and got enough sleep, you could cure anything. But Lorain didn't drink any milk, and she cried all night long, hardly sleeping even for an hour.

Dr. Mandelbaum filled the house with his importance. After he examined Lorain, he spoke to Mama and Papa in Yiddish. I could make out a few words but not enough to follow the entire conversation. When he left, I asked Papa, "Why doesn't Lorain's cold go away? Did Dr. Mandelbaum give you some medicine for her?"

Papa sighed. "Lorain doesn't have a cold," he said. "She has pneumonia."

I stood stunned. Pneumonia! That illness was the one that had killed Selena's grandmother. But the grandmother was an old, old lady, and Lorain was still an infant.

Dr. Mandelbaum came again on Sunday morning. This time I could understand his words. He said, "All you can do now, Rabbi, is pray." That advice was the kind that Papa was supposed to give people, not doctors. Of course, Papa prayed. He sat in a corner with a prayer book in his hand and read the verses half to himself and half aloud. Every few minutes he rushed to Lorain's little bed to see if she was still breathing. He looked as though he was checking to see whether or not God was listening, I thought.

Suddenly the idea occurred to me that perhaps Lorain was sick as a punishment from God because Betty had broken the Sabbath. And perhaps God was punishing me too, because I had known and hadn't told Papa and thus allowed Betty to repeat her sin over and over again.

Finding a chance to speak to Betty privately when everyone was crowded together inside the small house was hard. But finally I managed to confront her in the bedroom when no one else was nearby. "Do you think it is our fault?" I asked her. "Is God punishing us by making Lorain sick?"

"I don't believe in retribution. That's non-sense!" said Betty, flushing with anger. "If God would do a thing like that, he deserves to have every law broken," she said.

I winced. If God wasn't angry at us before, Betty's words would certainly give him reason for anger now.

Mama kept busy in the kitchen. Mrs. Fromberg had come to see if she could help, but there was nothing that she could do except sip tea and speak to Mama. As she listened, Mama kept her hands moving. She had done a laundry, rubbing the clothes in the big washtub. So she squeezed them dry and hung them on wash lines in the kitchen. Then she kneaded a batch of dough to make fresh bread. Having work to do kept

Mama's thoughts from dwelling on the fevered little body in the little bed.

At four o'clock, Papa suddenly put on his coat. "I'm going to the synagogue," he told Mama. "I will say the prayer; perhaps it will help."

I looked up from my library book. Papa's voice was sad and discouraged. I had never heard that tone in it before. "Papa," I asked, "can I go with you?"

Even without waiting for his answer, I dropped my book and rushed to get my winter coat. I put a warm woolen muffler around my neck and found my mittens, which I had left on the stove to dry when I had come in earlier.

Out in the street, it was already getting dark and was too cold to speak. My galoshes made squeaking sounds as I walked on the packed snow. The synagogue was near the lake, and the wind blew so sharply that it took my breath away. I held onto Papa's hand as we walked. I wanted to ask him about Lorain, but I didn't know how to phrase my question. Could it be that Lorain might die? Could it be a punishment from God? But death was for old people like Selena's grandmother or President Harding, not for tiny babies who hadn't had a chance to know the world.

When we reached the synagogue, I sat in one of the pews while Papa went up to the platform to join the other men assembling there. I counted seven men including Papa. I knew that they couldn't recite the prayers unless there was a minyan of ten men. In Jewish tradition, ten men are needed to hold a formal service.

I sat waiting and watching. For a long time, I kept my coat on until gradually my body began to thaw out and I felt the warmth of the room. Another man came and then still another. The men spoke among themselves as they waited. Only one more was needed, but the weather was bad. Sometimes they didn't get the minyan that they needed.

The door opened and Mr. Rabinowitz came in, coughing as he walked. Papa frowned. I knew he was thinking that Mr. Rabinowitz belonged at home and not out in the cold. But his wife had died a few months before, and so even though he was approaching eighty, Mr. Rabinowitz came every morning and every evening to recite the kaddish prayer for the dead. If his health permitted him, he would do so every day for a full year. The men put their prayer shawls around their shoulders and stood huddled together. They were ready to begin.

I opened a prayer book. I tried reading some of the Hebrew words. Papa had taught me the Hebrew alphabet, and I had learned to sound out many of the words, even if I didn't know their meaning. I knew Papa was proud that one of his daughters could read a little Hebrew. He always said that he would teach me more, but somehow there never seemed to be enough time. My eyes moved across the page, but my thoughts were not on the Hebrew letters. I kept thinking about Lorain.

When she was first born, I had been disappointed for an instant that she was not a brother. But from the moment that I had seen her, I had loved her all the same. I was too young when Evie was born to appreciate the wonder of life. Each finger and each toe on Lorain's body was a miracle, and I could watch her for hours without becoming bored.

If Lorain died, she would never learn to say her own name or to speak any words at all. She would never learn how to walk, never taste Mama's fresh bread, never read a single book, never play in the snow. There were so many things that one took for granted. Suppose one never smelled a flower. Suppose one never had a penny to go to the grocery store and pick out one of the flat chocolate creams in the box on the counter. Those little things were what made each day special: the sun shining, the scratchy feeling of Papa's beard. I sniffed and reached into my dress pocket for my handkerchief. Please, God, I prayed, don't let Lorain die. Let her live to be as old as Mama and Papa. Don't punish her for Betty's and my sins.

Papa came down from the platform. The

prayers were over. "Why are you crying?" he asked me.

"Oh, Papa," I sobbed. "Is Lorain going to die?" I rested my head on his shoulder, and my tears dropped onto the white silk prayer shawl.

"I will tell you what I did," said Papa, patting me softly on the back. "During the prayers, I gave Lorain a new Hebrew name. Now she is Chaia. Chaia means life, and her full name will be Chaia Lila Levin. Some people believe that by giving a sick person a new name they will fool the Angel of Death."

"Oh, Papa," I said, sitting up and looking at him, "what a wonderful idea." I smiled at Papa, and he smiled back at me. "Do you believe it will really work?"

"I don't know," he said, shrugging his shoulders. "But one must do everything one can."

"Oh, yes," I agreed. "Is there anything else we can do?"

"Yes," said Papa. "I've been thinking about this all day, and I'm going to do it right now."

Suddenly he jumped up and rushed out of the sanctuary area.

I followed him down the hallway toward his office. As I entered, I could hear him already speaking on the telephone.

"Is this Dr. Pelowski?" he asked.

I held my breath. Dr. Pelowski was the other doctor in the area that many of my classmates went to when they were ill. He wasn't Jewish. The Jewish people in town all went to Dr. Mandelbaum.

"This is Rabbi Levin speaking. My little daughter, five months old, is very sick. Could you come to see her? We live on Brownell Avenue," Papa said.

Dr. Pelowski must have agreed because Papa thanked him.

"Come," said Papa, hanging up the telephone receiver. "We must go home and tell Mama to expect Dr. Pelowski. Perhaps he will think of a remedy that Dr. Mandelbaum hasn't."

"Papa," I asked, "won't Dr. Mandelbaum be angry?"

"I imagine so," said Papa. "But we must do everything in our power to help Lorain, even if it makes Mandelbaum angry."

That evening as we were having supper there was a loud knock at the door. It was Dr. Pelowski. In every way he was the opposite of the Jewish doctor. One was tall, the other short. One was bald, the other had a full head of white hair. One was pompous and full of his own importance, and the other was quiet and gentle in his manner. Dr. Pelowski turned to Mama and Papa and said, "Let's try to give her the same medicine we would prescribe for an adult. It's dangerous for an infant, but it's our only chance. Dilute the dosage with an equal amount of water. It's a gamble, but we must take it."

"Yes," agreed Papa.

"Don't give her any milk to drink," he said to Mama. "Try a little fruit juice or water with sugar in it instead. I can't promise you a miracle, Rabbi," said Dr. Pelowski. "Miracles are for God. Mortals can only use their brains and their hands and do their best. But I've cured two other babies with pneumonia this winter, so perhaps I can cure a third."

His manner gave me a good feeling. I looked at Mama and Papa. They both seemed to like Dr. Pelowski too. For two days, Lorain still had her fever. But on the third day the fever dropped. Papa still prayed, but apparently the Angel of Death had been fooled. The medicine had worked!

"Which thing cured Lorain?" I asked Papa. "The medicine or the prayers?"

"Both," said Papa. He spoke with great certainty, and he was looking happy again. His shoulders didn't droop, and he hummed Yiddish melodies as he walked about the house. After supper, he took out his violin for the first time in several weeks, and he accompanied Abby when she played the piano. The gay music reflected the happy mood of all the family.

In the midst of the concert, there was a

knocking at the front door. I got up to answer it. Standing in the doorway was Dr. Mandelbaum. Unlike his son, he did not wait to be asked inside. He pushed past me and turned toward Papa.

"My price wasn't good enough? I didn't charge you enough money?" he shouted. "Twice I came out of my way to see the baby. But you didn't trust me, and you had to call in that goy!"

Goy is a word that means non-Jew, and I knew that Dr. Mandelbaum was angry that another doctor, and a non-Jew at that, was the one who had cured the rabbi's baby. I wondered how he had heard the news so quickly. Lorain was a small city, however, and there were very few secrets in it.

Papa laid his violin on top of the piano before he spoke. "Mandelbaum," he said speaking gently, "my wife and I will be forever grateful to you for the time you devoted to looking after the baby. You were very generous and helpful. But I couldn't not call Dr. Pelowski. If the devil himself had opened a medical office in town, I would have gone to him. I hope you can understand that."

Dr. Mandelbaum did not look as if he could understand at all. "Don't you ever call on me again," he threatened Papa.

"Mandelbaum, I hope to God that I don't need to call upon you or any doctor. No one ever wants to. Please, don't take this personally. It was something I had to do. Come," said Papa extending his hand, "join me for a cup of tea as friends."

"I am not your friend," said Dr. Mandelbaum, turning toward the door. It slammed behind him as he went out.

For a moment we all sat there stunned. Mama broke the silence. "Asher," she said, speaking to Papa in Yiddish. I could make out that she was upset because Papa had said that he would go to the devil. "The whole congregation will know of it tomorrow," she said.

"Yes," agreed Papa. "But I don't care if I lose my job. The important thing is that Lorain is well again." He picked up his violin and turned to Abby. "Come," he said, "let us continue with the music."

Abby's face was ashen. She shook her head. "I'm tired," she said.

Later I spoke to Papa. "If God is good," I asked him, "why does he make bad things like sickness and people getting angry at one another?"

"That is how life is," Papa answered, shrugging his shoulders. "Let me tell you a Chasidic story," he said. "There was once a man who took his two small sons to visit a wise and learned rabbi. The rabbi gave both boys a drink of beer. 'What is it?' he asked them. The first boy said, 'I don't know.' The second one said, 'It is bitter and good.' Then the rabbi turned to the father and said to him, 'Your younger son will grow to be a wise man.' You see, even at the age of three years, the younger son understood that something could be both bitter and good. And that is how life is," Papa said. "How could we appreciate the goodness of life without the bitterness too?"

Papa was right. Now that Lorain was well again, life was very good. I did not want to remember the bitterness of her illness, but it had made me realize how much I loved this tiny sister of mine, just as I loved Mama and Papa and all the others.

6

The Contest

Winter was passing. In the front yard, little yellow and purple crocus buds were poking out of the ground. Because it was our first spring in Lorain, we watched carefully to see what surprises the yard had in store for us.

"Flowers," I said, pointing to them so that Lorain would learn a new word. Of course, she couldn't speak yet. She was only seven months old. But her eyes followed my finger, and she smiled at the pretty colors. The late March wind blew fiercely off Lake Erie, and I pulled the woolen cap down on my head so it wouldn't blow away. Doris and I were taking turns pushing Lorain in the buggy. We held on tightly because the wind seemed as if it would blow the buggy away.

"Hi," a voice called out to us. It belonged to Selena Edwards, who was carrying a bundle of groceries for her mother. Despite the death of her grandmother, we still had not become best friends as I had envisioned. There was a constraint separating us, but whether it was the difference in our backgrounds or something else, I didn't know. Perhaps with time things would work out. Sometimes we walked to school together, and often Selena would play with me in the school yard during recess. Selena had gotten a C in arithmetic on her last report card. I felt the success was mine, but I knew that both Selena and Miss Peterson congratulated themselves on this wonderful improvement. Now she waved and walked on.

"Let's go in," said Doris. "I'm freezing."

"I am too," I said. "I wish someone would push me in a carriage with woolen blankets all wrapped around me."

"Someone did once," Doris reminded me.

"It's too bad people can't remember when they were infants," I said. But then I thought about Lorain, who was now strong and healthy. I was glad that she would never remember her pneumonia.

Inside the house it was warm and it smelled good. Mama had a pot of coffee on the stove, and the aroma filled the whole house. "Soon it will be Passover," she reminded us. "We will have a lot of work to do."

Passover is one of the most important of the Jewish festivals, and it required the most work and preparation. Every corner of the house had to be cleaned, and all the dishes packed away. Special dishes that were used only during the eight days of Passover were put in their place. "This year Evie will be old enough to help too," said Mama. She smiled at Evie. "I need every pair of hands I can get."

During Passover, Jews cannot eat any food that has been near hametz. Hametz is leaven, and it is avoided in remembrance of the hasty departure of the Jews from Egypt when there was no time for the bread to rise. In the days before Passover, all the Jewish families in town would be busy preparing for the holiday. But at our house there was another and even bigger job to do too. Papa always ordered the special Passover foods from New York City.

There were matzos, the flat crackers we would eat for eight days instead of bread, and matzo meal. There were also specially packaged containers of cinnamon, sugar, salt, and tea. Everything had been inspected and declared kosher for Passover. All these items were stacked in our house for the congregation to come and buy. Papa said that in big cities like New York and Chicago, where there were large Jewish communities, you could buy these items in a regular grocery store. But there were too few Jews in Lorain for any of the shopkeepers to be bothered with this special merchandise, and thus the job fell to Papa.

"If I wanted to be a shopkeeper, I would have married a shopkeeper," Mama joked. She said the same thing every year, in every town we ever lived in, as she counted out the matzos ordered by each family. She wasn't really complaining. Everyone knew that a rabbi's work was never done. Helping to fill stomachs with the proper food was just another task for him. But I noticed that with Papa away at the synagogue most of the time, the actual work fell to Mama and to us girls.

I tried explaining to Selena at school one day why I couldn't eat any milk or cheese or butter during Passover. "The people at the dairy don't have specially cleaned utensils," I said. "Perhaps the cans have contained leaven or perhaps the workers have eaten bread and not washed their hands properly. Since there is no way of checking it, the milk cannot be drunk by Jews during Passover."

"Well, cows don't eat bread. They don't even eat wheat," said Selena. "And so what if a bread crumb got into the milk can? You wouldn't even taste it. No one would know. So what difference can it make if a bread crumb is there?"

"God would know," I said. "He would know if a bread crumb was in the milk."

"It doesn't make any sense to me," said Selena.

I shrugged my shoulders. "It makes sense to me," I said. "I guess that's because I'm Jewish and you're not."

The first two nights of Passover we had big Seders, which are festive dinners. Everyone wore their best clothes, and Mama cooked special traditional foods like chicken soup with matzo balls and potato kugel. In addition to the family, Papa always invited a few members of the congregation to celebrate with us.

This year Papa asked Mr. Rabinowitz to join us. He also invited the Mandelbaum family. He meant the invitation as a peace offering, for he was sorry that Dr. Mandelbaum was still so angry that another doctor had been called in to care for Lorain when she was ill. But it was turned down. Dr. Mandelbaum did not want to forgive Papa. What was worse, Danny Mandelbaum wrote to Abby from Chicago saying that his father had forbidden him to continue to correspond with her or to see her anymore. Dr. Mandelbaum said he would not pay his son's tuition if he wrote to Abby.

"He's an ass. I never liked him," I told Abby. Danny seemed to be acting exactly the way Selena had when we first moved here. Both of them made and rejected friendships on the basis of what others told them to do.

Abby burst into tears and ran to the bedroom. She hadn't wanted to share her letter, but she couldn't keep it a secret when we all saw the postman deliver it and watched her read the contents.

"He's an ass. He's an ass," cried Evie, giggling.

"Evie, hush," Mama scolded. "And you too, Carrie. Don't say another word about this to

Abby. She and the Mandelbaum boy will have to settle the matter for themselves."

I felt sorry for Abby. She had suddenly lost the glow that had surrounded her. Now she always seemed on the verge of tears. She reminded me of the story of Romeo and Juliet, which I had read in *Tales From Shakespeare* that I borrowed from the library. That story had such a sad ending that I found myself worrying about Abby.

During the eight days of Passover, we had to make ourselves sandwiches of matzos spread with chicken fat for our school lunches. Unfortunately, the matzos turned soggy long before the lunch bell rang, and in addition I felt self-conscious eating my special meal while the others chewed away on fat sandwiches made with bread. I tried to pretend that I was living at the time of Moses and eating my meal in the desert.

At home, the meals never varied during Passover. There were matzos, vegetables, applesauce, and tea. Unless Papa killed one of the chickens, there was no meat. Sometimes I thought that I would never again have a soft slice of bread and butter or a piece of Mama's homemade cake. At night, I lay in bed thinking of a glass of milk. I wanted one so badly that I could imagine the cool whiteness of it against my tongue. Then I would feel guilty that I was thinking about food when Abby was lying in bed with thoughts that were so much more serious.

Then one day a wonderful distraction from the tedium of the Passover meals appeared. Overnight the town was plastered with posters announcing the arrival of a circus. I had read about circus life in a book called *Toby Tyler,* so the idea of having a circus right here in Lorain was very exciting. Everyone at school spoke about going.

"I wish we were rich enough so that we could all go," I said, as Doris and Evie and I stood admiring one of the posters on our way home

from school. It showed a picture of a woman in a fancy costume riding on an elephant.

"I want to go more than anything else in the world," said Doris passionately.

"Me too," said Evie.

On Friday afternoon, when the local newspaper arrived, it contained a full-page drawing of the circus. There were clowns, elephants, and acrobats. Children under twelve were invited to color in the picture and send it to the newspaper office. The fifty children who did the best coloring job would each be awarded a free ticket to the circus. The contest seemed like a miracle, only slightly less grand than the parting of the Red Sea. Perhaps we would see the circus after all!

The problem was that there was just one copy of the picture, and both Doris and I wanted to enter the contest. I wouldn't be twelve until June, and so I was still eligible.

"I want to go too," whined Evie.

"You're too little," said Doris. "You couldn't go alone." She turned to me. "Let's choose eeny-meeny-miney-moe to see who colors in the picture."

"No," I said, "I have a better idea." I ran to Mama to ask for two pennies to buy a second copy of the newspaper. "Then Doris and I could both color the picture, and we could both go to the circus," I explained.

"If you win," said Mama. But she had another suggestion anyway. "Instead of buying a paper, you can ask one of the neighbors for an old one after Shabbos is over."

Saturday passed very slowly. Doris and I were not permitted to color during the Sabbath, and so neither of us could begin work on the newspaper picture that we already had. We spent a lot of time studying the picture, however, and we discussed whom we could ask for the old newspaper.

"I know," I said. "Let's ask Selena. She had a birthday two weeks ago and now she's twelve, so she can't enter the contest."

I knew that Selena and her family came back

from church at eleven o'clock on Sundays, because I had seen them walking in the street together. So even though I was awake and dressed and ready, I had to wait until then before Doris and I could knock on Selena's front door. I had been there only once before, when I went with Mama to pay the sympathy call during the winter. Mrs. Edwards opened the door and invited us inside.

"We were hoping that you still have Friday's newspaper and that we could take it," I explained. "There is a contest for children under twelve, and since Selena is too old, we thought we could use your copy." Selena had two brothers who were both in high school, so they were too old for coloring pictures too.

Selena ran off to get the paper, but as she opened it to the picture, she started laughing. "I colored it anyhow." She showed us. "Even though I can't be in the contest, I thought it would be fun to do it." Doris and I looked at the picture, crayoned in with bright colors. I tried to be polite and say what a good job she had done, but I could hardly get the words out of my mouth. Besides, my brain was already thinking about whom else we could ask.

When we were out in the street again, Doris said, "Baby Artie wouldn't color in a picture."

I giggled. Baby Artie was our neighbor on the right. He was even younger than Lorain. His father was called Big Artie by everyone, and his pretty mother was Dell. We ran around the block to ring their doorbell. A dog was barking inside. When the door opened, a young puppy tried to run outside but was grabbed just in time by Dell. "Hi," she greeted us, as she pulled the puppy back into the house.

"We wondered if we could have your copy of Friday's newspaper," I asked once more.

"Sure," said Dell. Then she stopped. "I mean sure you could have if I hadn't already used it. Look at this." She pointed to the floor of the house. It was covered with newspapers. "Big Artie just brought home this dog for Baby Artie,

103

and we're having a terrible time getting him housebroken. So I put papers out on the floor to catch the puddles."

"Well, thanks, anyhow," I said.

"I hope you can train your dog soon," said Doris.

We walked down the steps from the porch and sat on our own porch. "Who could we ask now?" Doris wondered aloud. I shook my head. Finding another newspaper was much harder than I had anticipated. There were many other houses on the street, but we had only the barest nodding acquaintance with the people in them. First Mama had been busy with Lorain. Then it was wintertime and we were all indoors most of the time. So we hardly knew anyone at all. I felt much too shy to knock on strangers' doors, even though I wanted the newspaper badly.

"There's always Mrs. Fromberg," suggested Doris.

"She'll probably say that circuses aren't kosher," I said, but I jumped up from my seat.

Mrs. Fromberg was really our last chance. We hurried down the street to her house.

"I asked the others. It's your turn," I said to Doris, as we rang the bell.

"Meanie," said Doris, pinching me. The door opened. "Hello, Mrs. Fromberg. Do you have Friday's newspaper? There is a contest for children that we want to enter," said Doris, smiling sweetly at Mrs. Fromberg. I rubbed my pinch and laughed to myself. Clearly Mrs. Fromberg was charmed by the sweet voice that Doris was using.

"Come in, come in, and let me see," she said. "I think I used some of it to line the garbage pail." She made us sit down, and she gave us some candy that she had made especially for Passover out of carrots. We waited anxiously as Mrs. Fromberg left the room to look for the newspaper. I nibbled on the candy while we waited and gagged. "Carrots are vegetables," I said, "not candy."

Miraculously, the picture had not gone into

the garbage. We thanked Mrs. Fromberg quickly and ran off before she could cross-examine us about the picture and about Passover life at our house and certainly before she could ask us how we liked her carrot candy.

"Maybe it's a sign from God, a good omen, getting the paper on our third try," I said hopefully, as we ran up the steps of our porch.

"You read too many books," said Doris.

Maybe she was right, but anyhow now we could get down to the serious work of coloring in the pictures.

7

The Picture

After a long discussion about the merits of colored pencils versus wax crayons, we began to color our pictures. We worked very slowly so that not a single mark went outside the lines. I decided to use crayons, and Doris was using pencils.

Evie stood at the table, watching us. "I want to color too," she said.

I ran and got some blank paper for her. "Here," I said. "Now you can color too."

"No. I want a picture."

Doris pretended that she didn't hear Evie. She kept on coloring, but I got up a second time and looked through the old newspaper. I found an advertisement with a drawing of an automobile.

Evie looked at it with disgust. "There aren't any elephants," she said, pouting.

"Oh, leave us alone," said Doris, looking up. "How can we concentrate when you keep bothering us?"

Evie went sulking off to Mama, and Doris and I went on with our coloring. I felt very proud of my finished picture. Doris's picture was good too. I was sure that both would win prizes. We put the pictures on the kitchen table so that Papa could admire them when he came home.

Doris and I went outside and sat on the porch steps. The day smelled of spring, and it seemed to reflect our happy mood.

"Evie! What are you doing?" Betty shrieked from inside the house.

"I wonder what mischief Evie's got into now?" said Doris.

Before we had even a moment to speculate,

108

Betty called, "Doris, you'd better come inside."

Doris got up, and I followed her out of curiosity. There on the table were the two pictures. But instead of the neatly colored elephant and clowns, there were now red crayon lines running through Doris's picture. Evie had added her mark to the drawing.

"I hate you!" Doris screamed at her. "You are the worst little sister in the world." I stood there speechless, shocked at what Evie had done.

"What is happening here?" asked Papa, walking into the house.

"I hate Evie," Doris screamed again. "I'll never forgive her. Look what she did!"

Papa's face turned red as he looked from one member of the family to another. Mama explained that Evie wanted to color the picture and that she hadn't meant to ruin Doris's artwork.

Then Papa spoke. He did not scold; he never scolded. But he spoke in his most serious voice, the one he used when he delivered the sermons on the high holidays. "Evie, you must learn to respect the rights and the property of others. I am ashamed of you," he said, shaking his head. He turned to Doris. "As for you, I never want to hear you speak that way again to any of your sisters. I want my girls to protect and help one another. It would not be natural if there were never any misunderstandings among you. But I don't want you ever to hate one another. Don't say you do, and don't think you do. People are quick to use words like *hate,* but once something ugly is said, you can't retract it easily."

I looked at Doris and knew how she felt. If Evie had spoiled my picture, I would have said exactly the same thing to her. What she had done was terrible. How could Doris enter the contest now?

"I will get another paper," said Abby, kissing Doris.

"You won't be able to." Doris was sobbing. "We had a hard time getting this one."

110

"Let me try," said Abby, grabbing her sweater.

Forty minutes later she returned with a newspaper from Mrs. Osterman, her piano teacher. Supper was postponed while everyone stood around watching Doris. Slowly, carefully, she colored in the new picture while tears ran down her cheeks.

"Be careful, or you will get the paper wet," warned Mama.

"Rembrandt couldn't have done a better job," declared Papa, when Doris had finally finished. He gave us each an envelope for our artwork, and he promised to deliver the pictures to the newspaper office himself the following day after the morning prayers at the synagogue.

"Say a prayer that we win the tickets," Doris asked Papa.

"God is too busy to worry about circus tickets," Mama said, as Betty and she set the table for supper.

"God is never too busy," said Papa. "But I

don't know if his plan is for you to go to the circus this year. So you will have to wait and see."

I wondered if God kept a big black plan book the way Miss Peterson did at school. Did he write in it in Yiddish or in Hebrew? Maybe he used Aramaic as Papa did for the wedding ceremony. The question was interesting to think about.

Passover had ended and the regular dishes and foods were back on the table when the next Friday came. The week had been a long, long one as we waited for Friday and the contest results. But finally the day arrived. Doris and I grabbed at the newspaper when it came, and bumping our heads together we each tried to read the tiny print that listed the names of the winners. There was another paragraph that described the contest, but neither of us bothered to read it. The winning names were what was important.

"It's here!" I shrieked with joy. "Carrie Levin!" I had hoped so hard all week, and now my name was really and truly on the list. I would get to see the circus after all.

"Where's my name?" asked Doris.

We read down the list a second and a third time. "Your name isn't here," I said, looking sadly at her. "Maybe the newspaper didn't want to give two prizes in one family."

"That's not fair," said Doris. "I colored the picture two times. Mine was just as good as yours." She sobbed in disappointment.

My joy was gone. How could I go to the circus without Doris? I had won my ticket, but now I wouldn't be able to use it. I began to cry too. Evie watched us crying. "Is it my fault?" she asked, and she began crying too. For some reason, at that moment Baby Lorain, who seldom cried, began to howl too. She was probably teething. Mama went to pick her up. The door opened, and Papa walked in.

"Tears?" he asked. "Is that the way we greet

114

the Sabbath? Half my family is crying, and the rest looks sad too."

I held out the newspaper to Papa. "Doris didn't win a circus ticket. Her name isn't on the list of winners," I said.

Papa took the paper and sat down. He didn't just read the names as we did. He carefully read each word of the introductory paragraph. A smile crossed his face, and he looked up. "Listen," he said. Then slowly, clearly, in the deep, serious, synagogue voice that he had used a week ago, he read, "Four hundred and seventy-two entries were received. One of them was so outstanding that the editors have decided to award it two tickets to the coming circus production instead of one. This masterpiece of coloring was done by a girl who is ten and a half years old. Her name is Doris Levin."

Even before he read her name, we had all guessed. Doris was laughing and crying at the same time. Abby hugged her and began to hug everyone else too. Abby's delight in Doris's prize

115

seemed to be making her happy for the first time in many weeks. Betty and Evie and I joined in the shouting. Lorain stopped crying as suddenly as she had begun. Perhaps her gums no longer ached.

"Now this is how the Sabbath is supposed to be!" said Papa. "Joyous!" He blessed the wine and the bread, and the evening meal began.

"Doris?" Papa asked. "Who will you take to the circus with your extra prize ticket?"

Doris took a deep breath. "I've been thinking about it," she said. "I will take Evie. But she must promise never to touch one of my drawings or papers ever again."

"I promise, I promise!" shouted Evie. But then she added, "The second picture you made was better. If I hadn't colored on the first one, I bet you wouldn't have won at all."

"We'll never know," said Papa. "Besides, it doesn't matter. What matters is that you are all good friends again. And also that three of my children will be able to go to the circus and have a good time."

"It must have been God's plan after all," I said.

"And good coloring," said Doris proudly.

As it turned out, the circus was every bit as wonderful as we had anticipated. Our tickets were good for any performance of our choice, and so we planned to go on the following Sunday afternoon. At the last minute, Abby bought tickets for herself and Betty with money she had saved from her job at the pharmacy. So the five of us went off together. We rarely did things together anymore, but none of us had ever gone to a circus, and so we were sharing the new experience.

Mama sat out on the porch and waved good-bye to us. Lorain lay sleeping in the buggy.

"Too bad you and Papa and Lorain can't come too," I said.

"Lorain is too little, and Papa and I are too old," Mama said with a laugh.

But no one could ever be too old for a trip to the circus. Everything about it was wonderful:

the sights, the sounds, and the smells. The first things we smelled were doughnuts, frying in a huge vat of oil. They were being sold just inside the entrance, and they smelled delicious.

"Let's buy some," said Betty. These days she usually cared too much about her appearance to be attracted to food, especially doughnuts, so I was surprised.

"We can't," said Abby. "They may be fried in lard." Jews don't eat lard, which is fat from a pig. I suspected that if she were alone, Betty would not have been deterred by the thought of lard. I was glad that she didn't argue. This day was one for good times and no disagreements. Instead, we bought a large bag of roasted peanuts, which we shelled and ate as we walked about the sideshow and admired the tiniest man in the world and the fattest woman.

"I bet she eats lots and lots of doughnuts," whispered Evie, as we walked away from the woman. The sign said that she weighed 450 pounds.

We took our seats in the grandstand and

watched the parade of elephants, the acrobats, the tightrope walkers, and the clowns. All of them were dressed in colors more radiant than any that Doris or I had used in the pictures we had completed for the newspaper. All around us were other people applauding and enjoying the spectacle too. We recognized many from school and from the local shops and from the synagogue. Seeing them all in one place made me realize that even though we hadn't lived in Lorain for very long, I already knew—at least by sight—many of the faces. Lorain began to seem more like our true home, and I was glad to be part of the crowd, no different from anyone else.

Walking back to the house on Brownell Avenue in the early dusk, we talked about what we had enjoyed most.

"I liked the monkey dressed in clothes and riding on the dog," said Evie.

Doris and Betty liked the acrobats. Abby said simply, "I liked it all." I looked at Abby closely. The afternoon had been good for her. She really appeared to be her old, happy self again. The circus had taken her mind off that terrible Danny Mandelbaum, who was afraid of his father's shadow.

I reached out and took Abby's hand and squeezed it. "Me too," I agreed. "I loved it all. This was a perfect day, and I will remember it forever."

8

The Storm

Wherever we lived, one thing was always the same. Winter seemed to last forever, and when it finally ended and spring arrived, the new season lasted only a few days. Then it was summer, and we all sat about fanning ourselves and trying to recall the cold days that we had hated a few months earlier.

The last Saturday in June was dreadfully hot. From the moment I woke, I felt grumpy and uncomfortable. In the first place, I had developed a prickly heat rash around my neck where the nightgown had rubbed during my sleep. Even talcum powder did not make it feel better. Secondly, the milk at breakfast had turned sour from the hot weather. All the ice in the icebox had melted, and we wouldn't be able to get any more before Monday. And finally, it was Shabbos, which meant that there weren't too many things that I could do to distract myself from the awful heat. On the day of rest, we couldn't write or draw or color or sew. Abby couldn't play the piano. If only it were Sunday, Doris and I could have begged Mama for money to go see the new moving picture at the theater. That would have been the best way to forget the hot weather.

"Who would like to walk with me to the shul?" Papa asked, as he got ready to leave. But who had the energy to walk the blocks to the synagogue? I watched as Papa left and was glad that I didn't have to spend the morning sitting in the stuffy temple. Papa was wearing his black suit and carrying his prayer shawl in the little cloth bag that Mama had made for it. How awful to have to wear a suit, I thought. At the synagogue, Papa would put a robe on too. I wondered if he could take off his jacket underneath the robe. No one would know, except

God, of course. But surely he would understand about the heat. Papa walked slowly down the street. He had not been feeling well during the past few weeks.

Because it was Shabbos, there were no chores to be done except feeding the chickens. Doris and I started a game of anagrams at the kitchen table. Since we couldn't write on Shabbos, we kept score by putting pieces of paper in a book at the page number that indicated the number of points we had. Even though Evie didn't know enough words to play, she stood at the table, watching us. "Must you stand so close to us?" I complained. "There is hardly any air to breathe."

Evie walked away. Lorain was crawling on the floor. How lucky to be a baby, I thought, observing her. She was wearing only a diaper. She didn't seem to know that it was hot or that it was Saturday. Every day is exactly the same for a baby, I decided.

"Maybe it's cooler out on the porch," I suggested to Doris. I could feel the sweat dripping down my back under my dress. The day was going to be a long, long one. We moved our game, but on the porch I couldn't help being distracted by the children passing down the street with their towels over their arms and their bathing suits under their clothes. They were going to swim down at the lake. If only Doris and I could go too, I thought. But on Shabbos, Jewish children are not permitted to do such things. We could go to the library, but even it did not appeal to me today. It was too hot!

When Papa came home at noon, he looked flushed with the heat. He walked even more slowly than he had in the morning. "You should have stayed home. I knew you weren't feeling well," Mama scolded him.

"Tomorrow I will stay home," Papa said. "Today it was my duty to hold services."

"Duty!" shrieked Mama. "You owe nothing to those people." I knew she was referring to the members of the synagogue. Dr. Mandelbaum had announced to the board that he had no intention of voting to renew the rabbi's contract when it expired next year.

"Hush," said Papa. "My duty is to God and to my family. Now it is to my stomach. Aren't you going to serve me anything to eat?"

Papa knew that food would distract Mama from her concern for him. He needed to eat more than he had been recently. On the table were cold chicken and vegetables that had been cooked the day before. There was also bread that Mama had baked on Friday, but nobody ate much. It was too hot. When the meal was over, Papa and Mama retired to their bedroom for a nap. I thought that Papa napped more often these days than he used to.

I took my library book, *Anne of Green Gables*, and sat down with it out on the porch. I had already read the story once, but the afternoon hours would pass faster if I read it again.

"Read to me," begged Evie.

"Oh, Evie, I can't. It's so hot I can't make my voice work," I complained.

Abby had put Lorain down for a nap, but the

baby was restless. "I'm going to take Lorain for a walk," she said, putting the baby into the old carriage. "Come with us," she invited Evie.

I was glad not to be bothered anymore. Betty and Doris were reading too. The house was quiet. Only the squeaking of the carriage wheels as Abby and Evie walked away on the sidewalk interrupted the silence.

"It looks like rain," said Abby. "We won't go far, just around the corner and back."

I looked up from my book for a moment. She was right. I hadn't noticed it before, but the sky did seem darker than it had been earlier. In a short time Abby and Evie were back. Abby asked me to help her lift the carriage up onto the porch. Lorain had fallen asleep, and now it had begun to rain lightly.

"Perhaps the rain will cool us off," said Abby, wiping her forehead with her handkerchief.

"I wish we could go to the moving pictures," whined Evie.

"Don't be silly," said Abby. "This is Shabbos. Come, I'll read you a story," she said.

I watched them walk inside. Abby was always good. I knew that I should have offered to read to Evie, but it was so hot that I had no patience for doing good deeds. Even sitting on the porch while the rain drizzled down wasn't cooling, but I became so absorbed in my book that I didn't notice the weather or the time.

Vaguely I heard the murmur of voices from inside the house. Abby and Betty were setting the table for an early supper. The china dishes clattered sociably. I wondered why Betty had stayed home today. She usually said that she was spending Saturday afternoon with one of her classmates. In a sense she did, but what she never told was that they spent the time together at the theater.

I got up and walked into the kitchen. There on the table was a large bowl of strawberries and smaller bowls containing sour cream and cottage cheese. The red of the berries looked lovely against the white tablecloth. The light coming in the window had a greenish cast, and it gave everything a strange glow.

Abby put out cups for tea, and Betty was counting out the spoons at each place. I reached out my hand to take one of the berries.

Suddenly, from one moment to the next, a wind began to howl outside and the rain that had been drizzling gently began to fall in torrents. Abby rushed outside to bring in the carriage, which was still out on the porch.

Mama ran into the kitchen. "Hurry!" she shouted to us all. "Go down into the cellar. I will wake Papa." Her voice was shrill with fright. For a moment, I stood stunned. Then I grabbed Evie and pulled her along. Doris was behind us, and Betty too. Abby snatched Lorain from the carriage. The baby whimpered softly, not understanding why she had been yanked from her dreams.

Papa and Mama joined us in the little basement area. Even with the door to the kitchen closed, we could hear the fierceness of the wind banging shutters and breaking glass. There were enormous crashes of thunder too. All the noise was frightening.

128

"Thank God we are together," said Mama. "Thank God it is Shabbos."

I pressed close to her. I had never heard so much noise. The wind was so strong that it seemed as if the house would be blown away.

"Is this the end of the world?" Evie asked.

"Hush, hush," scolded Mama. "Don't talk nonsense."

Evie and Doris were crying. I had no tears in my eyes, but my breath came in gasps. I had never felt so frightened in all my life.

"Papa," I whispered, "say a prayer for us."

It was so dark in the basement that I couldn't see, but I felt Papa lift his hands and cover his head with them. He had jumped out of bed so quickly that for once his head was uncovered. He began to chant some words in Hebrew. I didn't know what they meant, but there was something in Papa's tone that made me feel better. He knew the language of God, and surely everything would be fine if he spoke to Him. He would tell God to stop the wind from blowing down our house.

"Amen," Papa concluded.

Everyone except Lorain echoed the word. "Amen."

For a moment we stood in silence. "Listen," I said. "The wind stopped. It really did."

We stood together, listening to the silence.

"Oh, Papa, you did it," said Doris. "You stopped the wind."

"I did not stop it," said Papa. "But I am glad it is over." He listened again. "It seems quiet. I will go upstairs and take a look," he said. "Everyone wait here until I call you," he added, when we started to follow behind him.

I stood waiting with my hands clenched into fists. Even though the horrid wind had ceased, I was still afraid.

Papa called from above. "I think it is safe to come up. Just watch where you step."

At the top of the basement steps, I took a deep breath. A horrible sight was waiting for us. In the dim light of the room, I could see that the floor was covered with broken glass and china. The wind had knocked out several windows, and where the table had stood so serenely just a few minutes ago there was now a rubble of shattered glass, broken chairs, and strawberries.

Lorain began to laugh. She didn't know what she was seeing. She didn't know enough to be afraid. "She thinks this is all a game," said Mama, taking the baby from Abby's arms.

"What happened?" Doris asked. We were standing by one of the broken windows and looking out into the rain and at the maple tree in Big Artie's yard. That tree that had been growing since before any of us were born had been uprooted. It lay half in the yard and half on Brownell Avenue. An automobile that had been parked on the street in its path was completely smashed. Our chicken coop was gone, and one lone hen was running about in the rain outside.

"What happened?" asked Betty, repeating Doris's question.

"Is this the end of the world?" asked Evie, for the second time in half an hour. "Is the Messiah coming?"

I shuddered, but whether because of Evie's words or the dreadful destruction all around, I didn't know.

"Nonsense," said Papa. "That was a tornado wind that just blew past us. But we are all well. *Baruch ha shem*. Bless the Lord. No one here was harmed."

"That wind was awful," I said. "I don't think I'll ever forget that sound. I thought the house would blow away. I always felt so cozy and protected in our house, but look at this." I pointed to all the rubble. "Even houses aren't safe. Suppose we had been eating supper." Then I broke into tears.

Lorain strained in Mama's arms. She tried to reach out for one of the berries that was on the floor. Somehow, although trees had fallen, a berry had managed to retain its perfect shape.

"Lorain is so lucky," I said. "She doesn't know what happened at all. She will never remember this day."

Papa put his arm around me. "Hush," he said. "The Lord looked over us. You are safe

and the storm has gone." He turned to Mama. "I must go and see if the members of the congregation are all well. Some may be hurt and needing help."

"Asher, you can't go out. You're not well yourself," protested Mama.

I looked closely at Papa. In the dim light his skin shone pale and sickly. There was more white in his beard than black these days, and he seemed very frail. Every hour Papa appeared to be aging by months; he was becoming an old man before our very eyes.

"I must go," said Papa firmly. "The people need me."

Evie started to cry. "Suppose the wind comes back," she said. "Who will pray for us?"

"I will always pray for you, wherever I am," said Papa, reassuring her and all of us.

"Take your coat," said Mama. "It's still raining." She seemed resigned to Papa's going outside.

"May I come with you, Papa?" I asked. "Maybe I can help too."

134

"I'll come too," said Betty. The two of us hurried out the door before Mama thought of arguments to keep us inside.

Outside the world seemed turned upside down. Trees were lying across the roads, cars were where cars had never been before, fences had been blown down. There were houses without roofs, roofs without houses, broken glass, smashed furniture, fires, people walking out in the street, people crying and shouting.

"It looks like the pictures in my history book of France during the Great War," said Betty softly.

"It's awful," I said, gooseflesh covering my arms. I grabbed Papa's hand.

"Careful," someone shouted to us. "The electric wire is down. The poles blew down in the storm."

A policeman stopped us. "There is a curfew," he said. "Everyone must go inside. No one is to be out on the streets."

"Curfew?" Betty asked.

"Yes," said the policeman. "There is looting

in some areas, and we're afraid that people will get hurt."

"I'm the rabbi," said Papa. "Rabbi Levin of Temple B'Nai Israel. I must go and see if the members of my congregation need help."

"I'll let you through, sir," said the policeman to Papa. "But these girls must go home."

I didn't know whether to be relieved or annoyed that the policeman escorted us back home. The streets were frightening, but I didn't feel in danger.

"A terrible tragedy happened in town," the policeman told us.

"Worse than all this?" I asked. I couldn't imagine anything worse than the damaged houses I saw around me.

"The balcony collapsed at the State Theater. It was filled with people watching the moving picture when the storm came and knocked it down. They were still counting the bodies when I left," the policeman said. "But I think at least seventy people were killed."

Betty and I both gasped. The policeman

seemed sorry that he had spoken. "It's all right. You're both safe," he said, as we reached our house. "Luckily, this part of town escaped the worst of the damage."

He turned and went down the street. Betty had her hand on the knob of the door, but I stopped her from opening it. "Oh, Betty!" I said. "Suppose you had been there. You often go on Saturday," I accused her.

"Well, I didn't go today!" she answered sharply, but I could hear the fear in her voice.

I threw my arms around her. "Oh, Betty, this is all so terrible, like a bad dream. I wish we would wake up."

Betty hugged me tight. "Shush," she said. "Mama will hear us. We mustn't upset her. Things are bad enough as they are." She was about to say more, but the door opened. Abby stood in the doorway holding a candle for light. It was a braided havdalah candle that under normal circumstances would have been lit at sundown to mark the end of Shabbos. "I thought I heard voices," she said. "Come in and tell us what is happening outside. The telephone lines must be down, because the phone is dead. I've tried calling the police and the newspaper for information, but I can't reach anyone."

We went inside. Mama was rocking Lorain on her lap. Evie was curled up on the sofa, asleep. Even though the Sabbath was over, two Sabbath candles were burning in their holders, giving the only light in the room.

Neither Betty nor I mentioned the tragedy at the State Theater. There would be time enough for that news when Papa came home. "It is awful outside," said Betty simply. That was enough.

"The street looks like a war," I said, sitting down beside Mama.

"Thank God we are all safe and well," said Mama. "It is a miracle. A true miracle."

Then she spit three times to ward off the evil eye.

9

Aftermath

A hundred years seemed to have passed since Passover and the circus. I thought back to those peaceful days of springtime. When would life return to its calm, normal flow? After the storm, nothing seemed real. Everyday activities that had always taken place were forgotten. The last classes at school were canceled, and the semester was concluded without the final assemblies and the awarding of prizes. Abby graduated from the high school without any ceremony at all. Children stayed home and helped parents clean up houses and yards and salvage what they could from the losses.

Compared to others, we were very lucky. Some people had lost the roofs of their homes while others lost the entire house, which was either destroyed by the winds or the fires that resulted from downed power lines and gas explosions. Worst of all were the losses of human life. Hundreds of people had been killed, including eighty in the movie theater. Among the dead were two Jewish girls whose families belonged to the synagogue.

"What were they doing in a movie theater on the Sabbath?" demanded Mrs. Fromberg. She had stopped by to see if Mama needed any help, but as usual she brought more aggravation than assistance. "It served them right," she said sanctimoniously. "God has punished them!"

"What are you saying?" Mama protested, as she put a clean diaper on Lorain. "Bessie was only twelve, and Evelyn was fourteen. And what about the seventy-eight other people who were killed at the same time who weren't Jews?" She paused to catch her breath. "It wasn't their Sabbath. Surely God wouldn't kill all of them just to punish two foolish girls."

"That's God's business," Mrs. Fromberg

said, shrugging her shoulders. "He knows what he is doing."

Mama didn't bother to answer. I watched her and saw how tired she looked. The tornado had taken a lot out of her. Last night Evie had wakened in the dark, crying from a nightmare. Mama had gotten up to comfort her, and when she lighted a small lamp, I wakened too. Mama was still wearing her daytime clothing. "Mama, why aren't you wearing your nightgown?" I whispered.

"Hush," Mama whispered back. "Never mind. I sleep in my dress in case I have to wake up suddenly for an emergency."

She didn't say anything more, but at that moment I became aware that even grown-ups like Mama were afraid. Life is uncertain and can be snatched or blown away unexpectedly in an instant. Under the covers, I shivered even though the evening was warm. A house would never again seem secure. Life was as delicate and uncertain as a burning candle. I had thought that death came only to weak people:

141

very old, like Selena's grandmother and Mrs. Rabinowitz, or very young, like Lorain when she got pneumonia. I had forgotten about the surprises, like President Harding's sudden death. Bessie, who was killed in the tornado, was only a little older than I was.

Papa agreed with Mama. He said that God didn't punish children for their errors; this is 1924, he said, not the biblical era. God is watching, but he won't send a plague or a flood to punish the world. He had given a sermon the week after the tornado, and he said, "Don't blame God and don't blame yourselves. When there is a calamity in nature, everyone is a victim, Jews and Christians, good people and bad. We can only continue to lead our lives and to hold on to our values. Be generous to your neighbors and loving to your families. Obey the commandments, one day at a time. No one, healthy or sick, young or old, ever knows how many days he has on earth, and so each day must be used well. Each day may be our last, but we must live it as if we are just beginning."

A month after the tornado Abby came home from work with an announcement that Mayor Hoffman was planning a rededication ceremony for the city. He was encouraging people to plant new trees to replace those that had been destroyed by the tornado. There would be speeches, the high-school band would play music, and there would even be refreshments.

We were glad to think of something pleasant for a change. After the storm, there had been much ill feeling, not only because of the tornado, but because of the hours of looting that had taken place afterward. For several days, martial law was declared by the mayor and the National Guard was stationed in the area.

Two days after Abby's announcement Papa received an official letter from the mayor informing him of the rededication ceremony and inviting him to give a speech. "Each of the clergymen in town will say a few words," Papa explained.

"Considering the small number of Jews in Lorain, it is a big honor," said Mama proudly.

"We will have to fix your good suit. You have lost so much weight your suit will look like a sack on you."

Doris and Evie giggled at the thought of Papa wearing a sack, but I noticed Betty and Abby exchanging worried glances. Papa had not been well before the tornado, but the days after the storm, when he walked through rain and mud puddles visiting the members of his congregation and comforting families on their losses, damaged his health even more. No one had eaten much after the tornado. No one had an appetite for food. But Papa, who already had lost weight during the spring, shouldn't have missed so many meals, worked so hard, and slept so little.

I had heard Mama speaking to Papa about his health. At her insistence, he had gone to see Dr. Pelowski. When he returned home, Papa spoke to Mama in Yiddish so I had to strain to understand. I wished Abby was home to decode the words for me. Her Yiddish was much better than mine. I gathered that Dr. Pelowski thought

Papa should be examined by a specialist. Papa's sister in New York was married to a doctor, and he would know whom Papa should see. "When the ceremony is over and life has returned to normal, then I will make a trip to New York," Papa promised Mama.

I felt greatly relieved, for I had faith in Dr. Pelowski. After all, he had helped Lorain last winter. If he thought a specialist could cure Papa, then no doubt he was right. So I looked forward with happy anticipation to the coming event; as soon as it was over, Papa would go and get his cure.

On a sunny August afternoon, as calm breezes gently moved the leaves on the few old trees that had escaped the ravages of the tornado, people gathered to rededicate the city of Lorain. Men who had temporarily lost their jobs when the shipyard was razed by the storm had been employed to clear all the rubble from the city. They had worked hard for this day.

Doris and I were wearing our matching Passover dresses with a blue-and-yellow print.

At the last moment, a button came off my dress.

Mama reached for her sewing basket, and she handed me a piece of thread while she began to sew the button back on. "Chew on the thread," she reminded me. There is an old superstition that if clothing is mended while you are wearing it, you will lose your memory. But the danger is counteracted if you chew on a piece of thread.

"Oh, Mama!" I said, laughing. "So much has happened since we moved to Lorain. I could never forget any of it." But to make her happy, I chewed on the piece of thread.

At last we were ready to leave. For the first time, Mama was bringing Lorain into the center of the city whose name she shared. Lorain was almost a year old now, and although she couldn't speak more than half a dozen words, she sat quietly on Mama's lap and watched alertly with her big, brown eyes. She seemed to understand everything going on around her.

"What a good baby," whispered a woman sitting behind Mama.

Mama turned around and said proudly, "She

is waiting for her father. He is next on the program." Mama was so proud of Papa sitting up on the platform that for once she even forgot to spit because someone had praised one of her daughters.

Papa looked very small standing on the platform. But his wonderful sermon voice came out loud and clear.

"Behold, how good and how pleasant it is for brethren to dwell together in unity!" said Papa, quoting one of the psalms from the Bible. I listened as he spoke about the good work done by so many hands to prepare for this day and contrasted it with the evil of the few during the hours after the tornado. I stopped listening and looked around me. There were so many people that I recognized. Again I felt, as I had the afternoon we went to the circus, that I really was a part of Lorain and belonged here. I hoped that Papa's quarrel with the synagogue board would be patched up. After all, many people had praised his devotion during the aftermath of the tornado. I liked Lorain, and I didn't want to leave. I looked at Baby Lorain sitting on Mama's lap, and I thought how lucky she was to share her name with this city. Perhaps someday I would go back to North Carolina and discover the things that had once made that place special for Mama and Papa.

Mrs. Fromberg was sitting across from us on the other side of the aisle. She caught my eye and nodded. Today even Mrs. Fromberg seemed a good friend. I had overheard a conversation in which she told Mama that she was trying to organize a campaign for Papa to remain at the synagogue.

There was a loud burst of applause, and I realized that Papa had finished speaking. Doris leaned over and whispered in my ear, "Wasn't Papa the best of all?"

Even though I hadn't heard all of his words, I knew that she was right. "Of course," I said. "Papa is always the best."

And we sat there smiling proudly as the people around us applauded Papa and nodded their heads toward us, the rabbi's girls.

10

Moving

According to the newspaper accounts, 300 people died and 1,500 people were injured by the tornado that last Saturday in June of 1924. But there was still another victim. I will always believe that the tornado was responsible for Papa's death, even though he didn't die until six weeks after the storm.

Dr. Pelowski said that Papa must have been ill for a long time. Perhaps he carried his illness inside him all the way from Rockford, just as we carried the milk and meat dishes. The disease was one that grew slowly and quietly, and probably for a while even Papa was not aware of its existence. But the stress and strain in the aftermath of the tornado drained Papa of his last reserves of strength before he had time to be treated by a specialist. He did not even have time to give himself another name, the way he gave one to Lorain. He was not able to fool the Angel of Death.

On a Sunday morning in August, a week after the rededication ceremony, Papa did not wake up. He had died in his sleep. For weeks after that day, every morning when I woke I forgot what had happened. Then suddenly I remembered, and Papa died once more.

One night I set the table for supper: plates, knives, forks, drinking glasses for everyone, and a clean cloth napkin folded on each plate. Betty carried the steaming pot of stewed meat and vegetables to the table, and we all sat down. Only as we were seated did I realize what I had done. I had set a place for Papa. We all sat looking at the empty place and crying. Even Lorain started to cry, though she was too little to understand the reason.

During the week of mourning, known as shivah, all the members of the congregation came to visit us. They brought food and little gifts, just as they had done a year ago when we first arrived in Lorain. The period was difficult. Papa, with his words of consolation, was the one who had always helped everyone, and now when he was most needed, he was gone. In the evenings, some of the men came to say the kaddish prayer. They were amazed when I stood beside them and said the words too. Even Mama was surprised. I knew then why that is a good prayer. There is a rhythm to the words as they are repeated that is soothing. I had often heard Papa say the words at the synagogue, leading the mourners. Knowing that these words had been said over and over again was reassuring. And just as I was saying them, so Papa said them when his own papa died. Someday someone will say the words for me:

Yis-ga-dal ve yis-ka-dash she may ra-bo. . . .
Magnified and sanctified be the name of God. . . .

152

The words made me closer to Papa. Sometimes I thought about the times when he asked
if I wanted to walk with him to the shul and I
said no because I was feeling too lazy. If only I
could have had a chance to walk with him just
one more time, to ask him just a few more
questions, to hug him and feel the bristles of his
beard against my cheek, just once again. But it
was too late. It could never be.

All day we had been wrapping dishes and
packing boxes. Once again we were preparing
for a move. This time we were going to New
York where Papa's sister and her family lived.
We would stay with Aunt Rose until we found
an apartment of our own. We had lived in so
many places that we shouldn't have been afraid
of another. But New York seemed so far away
and so big that I felt as if we would all be lost
there. Mama said that there were more Jews in
New York City than in all the other cities we
had lived in added together. Abby was going to
work in a shop owned by a cousin of Papa's, and

Aunt Rose wrote to say that she wanted to introduce Abby to several fine, handsome young men.

Betty had wanted to go to New York for years. Now that we were about to go, she was unhappy. "This isn't the way I imagined it," she said. "I wanted to go and make a big success in New York so that Papa could be proud of me. And now he will never know."

"Of course, he will," said Abby. "Don't you think he is looking down and watching us?"

Betty burst into tears.

The only one who was the same as ever, cheerfully crooning little tunes to herself and learning a new word almost every day was Lorain. She made us all laugh no matter how sad we felt.

Lorain was lucky not to be sad now, but she was unlucky too. She was so young that she wouldn't have any memories of Papa at all. I wouldn't have traded my sorrow for her ignorance. Mama said that we must all remember everything we could and tell Lorain about Papa when she got older. We had to give our memories to her. How ironic! All year I had envied Lorain that she was a baby without cares and memory, and now I felt sorry for her. She would never really know Papa.

But I knew that Abby was right and that Papa must be watching us, for he would not want to miss seeing his baby daughter grow up. She would have her first birthday far away from her namesake city, but we would not forget Lorain, Ohio. We would come back to visit the cemetery where Papa was buried and to see the new trees and lilac bushes as they grew taller. We would talk to our acquaintances about the old days and about the tornado and all the other things that happened here.

I didn't know if I would visit with Selena Edwards. She came with her mother to pay a sympathy call. "I'm sorry about your father," she said, "but I'm even sorrier that you are moving away. Now we will never send any messages back and forth with mirrors."

A year ago that thought had made me very

sad, but now such games seemed like pastimes for babies. A true friend is someone who cares about you and understands you and stands by you, no matter who you are and no matter what happens. Neither Selena Edwards nor Danny Mandelbaum were equal to that challenge of friendship. Someday I hoped to find a real friend, but for now I was lucky to have all my sisters. They were my friends, and we would always have each other.

We were leaving one friend behind, however. Poor Mrs. Fromberg would surely miss us, and we would miss her. Even I had come to appreciate her thoughtfulness and her concern for our family. She came every day during the shivah period and comforted Mama. She said such wonderful things about Papa that she made us glow with pride. Despite her ways that sometimes annoyed me, I knew that she was genuinely fond of us all.

By the time the train arrived in New York, it would be Rosh Hashanah once again. In New York, Aunt Rose would undoubtedly serve us a round challah to show that the year is a circle and that life goes on. This knowledge was something that Papa had given us all, and we would continue to move with the year and its seasons wherever we lived.

And each new year would be like the one that was just concluding, filled with days both bitter and good. I thought of the Chasidic story that Papa told me when Lorain was ill. How could we enjoy the goodness of life without the bitterness? Even something as terrible as a tornado was sometimes needed so that we could appreciate a quiet day.

Good-bye, Lorain, I thought. We would miss you, but we would have our Lorain with us.

Good-bye, Papa. We buried you here, yet we would carry you away inside us.

Yis-ga-dal ve yis-ka-dash she may ra-bo. . . .

ABOUT THE AUTHOR

Unlike Carrie in *The Rabbi's Girls*, Johanna Hurwitz has spent all her life in and around New York. She was born in the city and educated at Queens College and Columbia University. Formerly a children's librarian with the New York Public Library, Mrs. Hurwitz has worked in a variety of library positions in New York and Long Island.

The author recalls that when she was growing up her mother always shuddered when the wind blew. She complained that it was an awful sound. She couldn't understand why her mother was disturbed until she learned about the tornado of 1924. Many of the other incidents in *The Rabbi's Girls* also came from stories of the author's mother. Through imagination, conversation and research, after a while, Johanna Hurwitz actually began to feel as if she too had once lived in Lorain, Ohio.

These days, Johanna Hurwitz lives with her husband and two children in Great Neck, Long Island.